CHARLIE CALF

R. MACWHIRTER

Tellwell Talent
www.tellwell.ca

ISBN
978-0-2288-0277-8 (Paperback)

This book is dedicated to my father,
Gordon MacWhirter.

This is a short story about Charlie Calf
and a day in his life on the farm.

One warm spring morning, Charlie Calf awoke to find Momma Cow was not in the barn with him.

"I wonder where Momma went?" thought Charlie.

He stood up and had a big stretch and a big yawn.

Then, Charlie looked around, and there was Momma Cow. She was just outside the barn. Charlie went to the doorway to see her.

When he looked out, he felt the warm sun on his body. He called to Momma Cow.

"I'm hungry, Momma," he said.

"Well then, come over here and drink some milk," said Momma Cow.

Mammal: A type of animal that has hair or fur and provides milk for its young.

Nursing: When a young mammal drinks milk from its mother.

"How come you always have milk for me?" asked Charlie.

"Well," said Momma Cow, "as a **mammal**, some of the food I eat turns into milk inside my body. Then, that milk is ready for you to drink."

"That's awesome," thought Charlie, as he began **nursing**.

"Moo, I love you," said Momma Cow.

Charlie stopped nursing for a moment and said, "Moo, moo. I love you, too."

Charlie Calf finished his milk.

Then, Momma Cow said, "This is a big day for us."

"Why? What are we going to do?" asked Charlie.

"Today is the first time you will come to the **pasture** with me," said Momma Cow. "You will get to taste fresh green grass there. You will also get to meet many other calves and their mommas."

> **Pasture:** A place where animals can go to eat grass (usually a field).

Charlie was so excited. He began running and hopping around.

Momma Cow chuckled to herself. She liked seeing Charlie happy.

Charlie and his momma walked towards the pasture. He was a bit nervous, so he stayed near his momma. Charlie had never been this far from home before, but he knew his momma would keep him safe.

When they got to the pasture, the smells of fresh grass and **clover** were very strong. It all smelled so good, and it was green everywhere. Charlie put his head down to the ground and took a bite of grass.

Clover: A type of plant that cows like to eat.

Grazing: When an animal eats growing grass.

"Wow! This tastes great," he said.

"I like it, too," said Momma Cow. "And, when I eat it, I can make even more fresh milk for you to drink."

"This whole grass thing gets better all the time," thought Charlie, as he continued **grazing**.

Charlie stopped to watch his momma. She was not chewing her food very much before swallowing it.

"Momma, why are you eating so fast?" asked Charlie.

"Well, as **cattle** we are **ruminants.** We have four stomachs to digest our food," said Momma Cow. "We eat a lot right now and sort of burp it up later to chew it properly when we are resting. We call it chewing our **cud**."

Ruminants: A four footed mammal that chews its cud.

Cud: The food that a ruminant brings from its first stomach, back into its mouth, to chew a second time.

Cattle: Four legged ruminant animals with horns and hoofs.

Charlie thought that sounded kind of gross.

But, if Momma Cow said so, that was good enough for him. His momma knew everything.

After grazing awhile, Momma Cow said to Charlie, "Let's go for a walk and see who we can meet today."

"Yay!!" said Charlie.

They walked up a long hill. When they got to the top of the hill, they looked down the other side. Charlie could not believe what he saw.

Below them was a **meadow**. In the meadow, he saw cattle. There were many big cows like his momma and little calves just like him. Charlie could feel his little heart beating so fast.

> **Meadow:** A piece of grassland or lowland near a river.

"Momma, can I run down and play with the other calves?" asked Charlie.

"Of course, but you must come to me right away if I call you," said Momma Cow, as she gave him a kiss.

"You got it, Momma," said Charlie, as he took off down the hill.

Charlie raced down the hill to join the rest of the **herd**. He was so excited, he did not realize how fast he was going.

Suddenly, he tripped and fell.

He rolled over a few times and ended up flat on his back. When he opened his eyes, he saw a face really close to his.

"Are you okay?" asked the face.

"I think so," said Charlie, as he stood up and shook himself off. Charlie could now see another calf beside him.

"My name is Jewels," said the other calf. "I'm a **heifer**, a girl calf. What's your name?"

> **Herd:** A large group of animals that live and eat together.
>
> **Heifer:** A young female cow before she has a calf.

"I'm Charlie," he said.

"Where is your momma?" asked Jewels.

"She is at the top of the hill. She told me I could come and play," said Charlie.

"Well, what are we waiting for? C'mon, let's go play with the others," said Jewels.

Charlie was so happy to have a new friend.

Charlie and Jewels spent the next few hours playing and running with the other calves in the open field.

"This is so much fun," thought Charlie, as he ran around kicking his heels in the air.

Then, he bumped into a much bigger and older calf who was not playing with the other calves.

"WATCH WHERE YOU ARE GOING!" said the big calf. Then, he pushed Charlie to the ground.

No one had ever been mean to Charlie before. Charlie started to cry. His feelings were hurt.

Jewels came running over. She saw the whole thing happen.

"Why did you do that to Charlie?" asked Jewels.

"He bumped into me," said the big calf.

"It was an accident," said Charlie.

"Charlie's right," said Jewels. "I saw the whole thing. Pushing Charlie was not a nice thing to do."

This made the big calf embarrassed.

"I'm sorry for bumping into you," said Charlie.

"I'm sorry, too," said the big calf.

"I have an idea. Why not come play with us?" said Jewels. "What's your name?"

"I would like that," said the big calf. "My name is Sid. Nobody has ever asked me to play with them before."

Just before running off to join the other calves again, Charlie said, "Thank you, Jewels."

"You're welcome," said Jewels. "That's what friends are for."

Charlie, Jewels and Sid played together for a while. Jewels introduced Charlie and Sid to many other momma cows and calves. Soon, Charlie began to get tired.

"I would like to take a nap. Where can I sleep?" Charlie asked Jewels.

"You can sleep anywhere in this field, as long as your momma can see you," said Jewels.

So, Charlie lay down on the grass and soon was fast asleep. He awoke feeling a very strong wind on his body. When he stood up, the wind was so strong it knocked him down.

Charlie got scared. He did not know what to do. He called to Momma Cow.

Tornado: A fast turning column of air.

Shelter: A place that gives protection from bad weather or danger.

"Momma, help!" he yelled.

Somehow, Momma Cow was there with him right away.

"Get up, Charlie," Momma Cow said. "There's no time to lose. We have to run to the forest to find **shelter**. A **tornado** is coming, but don't worry. I will be beside you to block the wind. Let's go!"

Charlie got to his feet. The wind was still really strong. Even though he was shaky and afraid, he did what he was told. Charlie began running with his momma toward the forest. He could see many other momma cows and calves beginning to gather there.

Momma Cow was right beside Charlie every step of the way. Because she was so big and strong, the wind could not knock Charlie over again.

When they reached the forest, Charlie saw all the mommas were forming a circle.

"What is happening?" yelled Charlie, over the roar of the wind.

> **Shield:**
> Something that is used to defend against attack.

"We are making a **shield** for all the little calves," yelled back Momma Cow.

Charlie watched. After all the momma cows and calves reached the forest, the mommas grouped all the calves together. Then, the mommas finished their tight circle around Charlie, Jewels, Sid and all the other calves.

Now, Charlie understood.

The momma cows were all working together to keep the little calves safe inside the circle.

Branches and small rocks were flying everywhere. Even small trees were being knocked down.

The wind got stronger and stronger, but it could not move any of the cattle because the big momma cows were all working as one. They were pressing tightly together in a circle with the little ones in the middle.

Charlie was less afraid now, because he trusted the momma cows to keep him and his friends safe.

The wind lasted a short time. Then, it passed and was gone. Charlie felt a nose close to him. It was sniffing him. He looked up and saw it was Momma Cow.

"Why are you doing that?" asked Charlie.

"The wind blew dust in my eyes," said Momma Cow. Right now I can't see very well. But, I can tell you are my calf by your **scent**."

"Wow," thought Charlie. "I have so much to learn."

| **Scent:** Something that can be smelled. |

Just then, Jewels came over to Charlie.

"Are you okay, Charlie?" asked Jewels.

"Just a bit shaken," said Charlie.

"Me, too," said Jewels.

"We are all going back to the barn for the night now," said Momma Cow. "You should go to your momma, Jewels. I'm sure she's looking for you."

"Okay. See you later, Charlie," said Jewels.

"Bye," said Charlie, as he began walking back to the barn with Momma Cow.

As they were walking, Charlie thought about all that happened that day. When they were almost at the barn, he asked Momma Cow, "How did you know what to do when the wind started?"

Momma Cow thought for a moment and then said, "It's **knowledge** nobody teaches us. We are born with it. It's called **instinct** and almost all animals have it. When there is danger, our first thought is to protect our babies, no matter what."

Knowledge: Knowing or understanding something.
Instinct: Most often a fixed pattern of behaviour in animals.

"But you could have been hurt trying to help me today," said Charlie.

"Yes, but when we act on instinct in a dangerous situation there is not always time to think, only act," said Momma Cow. Now, let's get some rest. Tomorrow is another day."

Charlie and Momma Cow went into the barn. Momma Cow found them a dry place to lie down.

"Goodnight," said Charlie.

"Moo. I love you," said Momma Cow.

"Moo, moo. I love you, too," said Charlie.

The End

CPSIA information can be obtained
at www.ICGtesting.com
Printed in the USA
LVHW070121140819
627587LV00015B/79/P